Shoshana and the Native Rose

By Robin K. Levinson

Gali Girls Jewish History Series

Published by Gali Girls Inc.
Copyright © 2006 by Gali Girls Inc.

Published by
Gali Girls Inc.
48 Cranford Place
Teaneck, N J 07666

Please visit our website at www.galigirls.com

Library of Congress Cataloging-in-Publication Data

Levinson, Robin K.
  Shoshana and the native rose / by Robin K. Levinson.
     p. cm. — (Gali Girls Jewish history series)

  Summary: In 1662 in the colony of Nieuw Amsterdam, Shoshana Levy befriends a
Lenape Indian girl, but her mother reacts with horror, exhibiting the same prejudice
against the Indians that she herself has been subjected to as a Jew.
  I S B N 0-9773673-2-0
  1. Jews—New York (State)—New York—History—17th century—Juvenile fiction.
[1. Jews—United States—Fiction. 2. Delaware Indians—Fiction. 3. Indians of North
America—New York (State)—Fiction. 4. Prejudices—Fiction. 5. New York (N Y)—
History—Colonial period, ca. 1600-1775—Fiction.] I. Title.
  PZ7.L57967Sh 2006
  [Fic]—dc22
                              2006031202

                       I S B N 0-9773673-2-0

                   10 9 8 7 6 5 4 3 2 1

Contents

ACKNOWLEDGMENT

A sincere thank-you to Rachel Frankel, M.A., and Naomi Caldwell, Ph.D., for reviewing this manuscript before publication. Their critical commentaries and insights greatly enhanced this book's authenticity and educational value. Ms. Frankel is a recognized authority on the history and sites of colonial Jews of the Americas. An independent scholar and architect with a practice in Manhattan, Ms. Frankel has an undergraduate degree in history from Duke University and a Master of Architecture degree from Harvard University's Graduate School of Design. Dr. Caldwell, a member of the Ramapough/Lenape community, is an assistant professor in the Graduate School of Library and Information Studies at the University of Rhode Island.

A special thanks to glass artist and designer Roger Nachman, owner of Roger Nachman Glassworks in Seattle, Washington, for reviewing part of this manuscript.

CHAPTER ONE

VOYAGE TO THE UNKNOWN

"Tell me a story, Mamma. Tell me about the time we got attacked by pirates!"

"I've told you that story already, Shoshana."

"But I want to hear it again. Pleeease?"

"OK, OK, my beautiful rose. One more time, then right to sleep."

Shoshana Levy's mother, Rivka, slowly lowered her very pregnant body onto the bed. She swept the brunette bangs from her daughter's large brown eyes, which glowed and flashed like a cat's in the candlelight. Everyone agreed that Rivka was the best storyteller in Nieuw[*] Amsterdam. Her vivid descriptions captivated the children who lived in the Dutch colony, a colony that would be taken over by the British a few years later and renamed New York.

---

[*] *Nieuw* is the Dutch spelling of "New."

Rivka smoothed her gingham dress, cleared her throat, and began:

"We were sailing on a little ship called the *Falcon*. Our destination was Amsterdam, where we lived before moving to Recife, Brazil."

"When did the Dutch take over Brazil?" Shoshana asked.

"In 1624. Before that, the Portuguese were in charge. They made it against the law to be Jewish. Jews who lived there had to convert to Christianity and even so, these new Christians continued to be punished for not being 'pure' Catholics. But when the Dutch took charge, everyone was granted religious freedom. Many New Christians who were living there, including your grandparents, converted back to Judaism. With

Brazil suddenly a nice place for Jews to live, your grandparents invited us to join them there.

"How long did the Dutch rule in Recife, Mamma?"

"Almost twenty-five years," Rivka said wistfully. "During that time, the Jewish population flourished. By the time you were born, about five thousand of us were living in Recife. Pappa's sugarcane business grew into one of the biggest in Brazil. Our community even had a synagogue. Then, in January of 1654, the Portuguese took back control of Recife, and everything changed for us."

Rivka fought back tears as she remembered their happy life withering like a leaf on the forest floor.

"The Jews were given three months to sell their homes, pack their belongings, and get out," she said.

The *Falcon* was one of sixteen Dutch ships that carried the Jews out of Recife. It set sail on February 28, 1654. Shoshana, her parents, and her sister were among the twenty-three Jews on board. A few of the ships took the Jewish refugees to Caribbean islands or Central America. But most went back to Amsterdam, Rivka told her daughter.

"Amsterdam is the capital of Holland," Shoshana pointed out.

"Correct. That was our destination, too. But a squall blew our little *Falcon* off course just a few days into our voyage. We were running out of drinking water and food, and some of our sails needed mending. So our captain planned to drop anchor off Jamaica, a large

island in the Caribbean Sea. We hoped to replenish our supplies with coconuts and bananas, as well as fresh water.

"You, me, and baby Bina were on the back deck. You were tucking your doll, Muñeca, into her cradle. Do you remember that?"

"Not really," said Shoshana, who was only three years old at the time. She glanced over at Muñeca. Though a bit tattered, Shoshana's only doll occupied a place of honor, along with a book of Psalms, on the only shelf of her tiny bedroom.

"What happened next?"

"Suddenly, we heard a thunderous bang and *crrrrack* coming from the bow of the ship. The whole vessel

5

shook. You were so scared that you dropped Muñeca and ran into my arms. Your father told us to stay put while he went to investigate."

"Pappa is so brave!" Shoshana interjected. Her father, Akiva Levy, was more than brave. He was a man of great compassion and a born leader.

"Then what happened, Mamma?" Shoshana asked excitedly, as though she was hearing the story for the first time.

"When your father reached the bow, he saw that a cannonball had ripped a hole right through the deck boards. Seawater was rushing in. Pappa and several others grabbed buckets and started bailing out the water. Meanwhile, the rest of us rushed around searching for anything that might be used to plug up the hole. Before we knew it, the ship that shot the cannonball sailed right beside us—and it was manned by *piratas**! The *piratas* told us they were 'privateers.' They said their government gave them the 'right' to attack us and any other ship they wanted to loot. We didn't care what their government said. To us, those *piratas* were nothing more than thieves."

Shoshana snuggled closer to her mother, who wrapped her arm around her protectively before continuing.

"Using rope ladders and planks to link up our two

---

* *Piratas* is Ladino and Spanish for pirates.

6

vessels, the *piratas* forced their way onto the *Falcon* and ordered all of us, even the children, to lie face down on the deck."

"That part I remember! I got a splinter in my knee," Shoshana said. "Mamma, why didn't Pappa and the others try to fight off the *piratas*?"

"We had only a few guns on board, and they were no match for the *piratas*' weaponry. In addition to cannons, the *piratas* wielded swords and guns far more powerful than ours."

Next, Rivka told of how they stole all the money and jewelry they could find from the passengers before emptying the ship's hold of anything that could be sold.

"They took our extra clothing, shoes, pots and pans, candles, soap, pillows, almost everything we had," Rivka said. "If I hadn't put Muñeca in my dress pocket, they probably would have taken your doll, too."

Rivka took a deep breath and let it out slowly to calm herself before telling the next part of the story.

With swords at their backs, the *Falcon*'s four men, six women, and thirteen children, along with her captain and crew, were placed in a rickety rowboat and sent adrift in the tepid, blue-green waters. The rowboat had several tiny leaks, however, and it wasn't long before it would have to be abandoned. Fearing her whole family would drown, Rivka began to panic, until she realized that they were within a short swimming distance of Jamaica. Her husband hoisted Shoshana and her baby sister onto an empty wooden barrel that he'd managed to push off the *Falcon* during the melee. With one hand on Shoshana's back and the other on the baby's, Akiva and Rivka kicked with all their strength until they made it to shore. Akiva immediately grabbed the barrel and ran back into the surf to help the others. He did this several more times until everyone was rescued.

Sopping wet and penniless, but grateful to be alive, the castaways watched helplessly as the pirates returned to their ship and fired two more cannonballs into the starboard side of the half-sunken Falcon. As the ship's three masts slipped below the surface, the Jews felt as lost as the driftwood that was strewn all over the beach.

They were wringing out their clothes and dumping water from their shoes when a French frigate called the *Saint Catherine* appeared, seemingly out of nowhere, and chased the pirates away. On the beach, the Levys and the other families jumped up and down, screaming and waving their hands wildly to attract the warship's attention.

"Then what happened?" Shoshana asked breathlessly.

"For that, you must wait until tomorrow night, my beautiful rose," said Rivka, looking tired. She blew out the candle on Shoshana's bedstand, tucked her in, and kissed her goodnight.

The run-in with those dreadful pirates was one link in a chain of misfortunes that the Jews of the *Falcon* would experience in their quest to regain a home and religious freedom.

CHAPTER TWO

NIEUW AMSTERDAM, BRIGHT AND DARK

The next morning, Shoshana was jolted out of a fitful sleep by a nightmare featuring pirates and sand. The sun was nearly up. She dressed quickly and walked out to her front stoop. Surely the dazzling sight of the horizon glowing pink, then orange, then yellow would push that awful dream out of Shoshana's mind.

The Levy house stood at the highest point of a street that draped like a ribbon over a gentle hill, providing a beautiful panoramic view of Nieuw Amsterdam. Shoshana lived in the capital of Nieuw Netherland Province, which stretched over a region that, a few generations later, would become part of six states: New York, Pennsylvania, New Jersey, Maryland, Connecticut, and Delaware.

Nieuw Amsterdam was situated at the toe of a sock-shaped landform that jutted out between two large rivers. A canal split the city in half. The newcomers

from Holland had built many footbridges over the canal. They also dotted the cityscape with windmills to power the grain and sawmills, which were essential to their emerging colonial fortress town.

The cobblestone streets of Nieuw Amsterdam were arranged in a triangular grid, like a slice of a spider's web. The residential area featured wide sidewalks where neighbors liked to socialize while their children played games such as hoop and stick, hopscotch, and leapfrog. The houses, about 1,000 of them, were built closely together. Some had two floors, others just one. All had pointy red roofs, like the houses back in Holland. Light-gray smoke twirled out of every chimney.

Shoshana surveyed the district where blacksmiths, wheelwrights, candle makers, cobblers, and other tradesmen worked. She could also see huge trade ships with their billowing sails gliding in and out of the colony's bustling harbor. To her left were small farms and an apple orchard. To her right, the bright white steeple of the community's church poked into the sky. Shoshana shared the church with the town's other children when she attended classes since the building doubled as a one-room schoolhouse.

Also from her stoop, if Shoshana stood on tiptoe, she could see Fort Amsterdam, its thick walls curving around the easternmost perimeter of the colony.

All able-bodied men in Nieuw Amsterdam took turns standing guard at the fort. Soon it would be Shoshana's father's turn. Most of the men considered guard duty a burden. Not Akiva Levy. He embraced this responsibility because he had to earn it.

When they first arrived, the Jews were not allowed to do what all the other inhabitants of Nieuw Amsterdam took for granted: sell goods, own property, and participate in local government. The Jews also did not serve in the militia, which included guard duty at the fort. Instead, they were charged a special tax.

Time and time again, Akiva spoke to Governor Stuyvesant and the other local leaders on behalf of all the Jews in the colony. Akiva was well aware of the struggles to establish order in Nieuw Amsterdam so that it would be profitable for both the colony and Holland. Akiva told the leaders that the Jews wanted to help protect the colony and expand trade and commerce. "Jews could provide a wide variety of goods and services if given the opportunity," Akiva promised.

Over time, the Jews won the same rights and responsibilities that everyone else had, with one exception. They still weren't allowed to practice their religion openly; only Christians could do that. Nieuw Amsterdam's minuscule Jewish community had no choice but to worship in their homes, behind closed doors. The families took turns hosting Shabbat services, using a Torah scroll given to them by the synagogue across the sea in Amsterdam. When the community needed to move their Torah to another house, they hid it under a large blanket to avoid attracting unwanted attention.

"If the ancient *Israelitas*[*] could move a whole tabernacle from place to place in the desert for forty years, we can move our Torah from house to house," Akiva was fond of saying.

The Jews named their homeless congregation Shearith Israel, which means "remnant of Israel." Although they were still trying to gain permission to build a synagogue, the congregation was allowed to buy some land for a Jewish burial ground two years after their arrival in Nieuw Amsterdam. For Jews, establishing a burial ground demonstrates a sense of permanence in a new land.

From her house, Shoshana could not see the cemetery because it was on the outskirts of the city. Beyond it, a dense forest stretched out seemingly with

---

[*] Sephardic term for Israelites.

no end. In February and early March, when the snow began to melt, Shoshana could hear the *shhhhhhhhhh* of a rushing creek off in the distance whenever she stepped into the forest. Although she was curious to see the source of that sound, something else had always made her far more curious.

In Hebrew, "Shoshana" means "rose," but Shoshana had never seen one. Shoshana knew that names are very important in Judaism. A name represents a reputation. "If you destroy a man's reputation, you take away his good name," her father once told her.

Jewish names also carry the weight of history. In the Torah, Abram's name was changed to Abraham after he encountered God. Jacob was renamed Israel after dreaming that he was wrestling with an angel. Jews often gave their children Biblical names. The Jews of Recife were Sephardim, or Spanish Jews, who commonly named their children after living relatives as a sign of love and respect.

Names might also represent positive traits that parents want for their children. For instance, the male name Lavi means "lion" in Hebrew, which suggests strength. Ahuva, a girl's name, means "beloved." Shoshana's sister's name, Bina, translates into "wisdom." Akiva means "protect." Shoshana's name conjured up the rare beauty of a rose.

If a name is part of a person's identity, how could Shoshana understand the beauty of a rose without having touched her namesake or inhaled its perfume?

With no firsthand knowledge of roses, Shoshana felt
incomplete, like a puzzle with a piece missing. "Would
it always be this way?" she wondered.

Shoshana doubted she would even recognize a rose
if one dropped into her lap. Someone told her that a
rose's aroma was irresistible, like nothing else on earth.
Another person said there were rose species that bore
no scent at all. Roses could be deep carmine red, orange-

red, dark or pastel pink, yellow, light orange, or white.
Some sported generous, velvety blossoms with twenty
or more overlapping petals. Others had just five or six
small round petals that opened widely to reveal a vivid
yellow center.

The only thing that almost all roses seemed to
have in common were sharp thorns on their stems. The
thorns kept hungry herbivores away and discouraged
destructive insects. Only flying insects, such as wasps,

could comfortably sip rose nectar without being injured, Shoshana guessed.

As the sun floated over the harbor, she tried to imagine what a real rose might be like. "Maybe God borrowed the colors of the sunrise and sunset when He created my flower," she mused. "I wonder if its petals are softer than fur on a kitten's ear."

After the sunrise, Shoshana embarked on a fairly typical day. She helped her mother prepare breakfast and dress her four-year-old twin brothers. Then she and eight-year-old Bina walked the two miles to school. After the closing bell, she visited Mr. Winchell, the glassblower, whose daughter, Christa, was her best friend. By four o'clock, Shoshana was back at her house, immersed in homework.

Later, she helped her mother peel potatoes and slice carrots for that evening's stew. Akiva kissed his wife and children good-bye and left the house right after dinner to begin his overnight guard duty at the fort. After dinner, while Shoshana cleared the table, Rivka helped the younger children prepare for bed. Finally, it was Shoshana's turn for her mother's undivided attention.

"Tell me what happened after the *Saint Catherine* rescued us from the beach in Jamaica," Shoshana pleaded.

"We were delighted to be saved, of course, but the *Saint Catherine* was not headed to Amsterdam; it was

headed here, to *Nieuw* Amsterdam. At first, we were upset that we would not be reunited with our friends from Recife. But the Saint Catherine's captain, Jacques de la Motte, told us that people of many different religions were living in Nieuw Amsterdam. You see, the colony was under the control of the Dutch West India Company and, like the Netherlands, was tolerant of different beliefs. So, we naturally expected to be welcomed here, too.

"The trip northwest over the Atlantic Ocean seemed to take forever. Fortunately, there was enough food and sleeping space on the *Saint Catherine* for all of us. About seven months after we left Recife, on the day before Rosh Hashanah, in fact, we sailed into Nieuw Amsterdam's harbor."

"Were we excited?"

"Yes, very excited. The idea of beginning our *new* lives in a *new* land called *Nieuw* Amsterdam on the Jewish *New* Year was thrilling. But when we tried disembarking from the Saint Catherine, Captain de la Motte demanded payment—2,500 golden guilders—for the sleeping quarters and the food he'd given us during the voyage. He did this even though he knew the *piratas* had stolen almost everything we owned, including most of our money. To make matters worse, Nieuw Amsterdam's governor, Peter Stuyvesant, didn't even want us to live here."

Shoshana was confused. Her mother had never gotten this far into the story before because she thought Shoshana was too young understand; but she was almost twelve now, practically a young woman. Rivka went on to explain that two Jewish men who had arrived from Holland just a few weeks before tried to help by donating money and some of their valuables, but it wasn't enough to meet Captain de la Motte's price.

To Governor Stuyvesant, two Jews living in his community were quite enough. The idea of twenty-three more moving in alarmed him. "He said our religion was 'abominable,'" Rivka said. Anticipating Shoshana's question, she quickly added, "Abominable means 'terrible.'"

"What's so terrible about being Jewish, Mamma?"

"Nothing, of course. You see, Shoshana, our beliefs and practices are not the same as Christian beliefs and practices, and the vast majority of Europeans and colonists are Christians. Too many of them don't like us because we are different. They make assumptions about Jews that aren't true and teach their children to hate and fear us. It's a vicious cycle of prejudice that is very hard to break."

"Oh, so that's why we have to hide the Torah scroll under a blanket when we move it from place to place," Shoshana said.

"Yes, that's right."

"Governor Stuyvesant sure is scary."

To the children of Nieuw Amsterdam, Jewish or not, Governor Stuyvesant *was* a fearsome figure, with his thick, dark mustache and large sword dangling from his belt. In 1644, his right leg was crushed by a cannonball during a battle with the Spanish, and the limb had to be amputated. In its place he wore a silver-tipped wooden peg, which is why some people called him "Old Pegleg."

Rivka told Shoshana about the nasty letter Governor Stuyvesant wrote to his superiors at the Dutch West India Company, which oversaw the colonies on behalf of the Dutch government:

> *We have deemed it useful to require the Jews in a friendly way to depart; praying that the deceitful race be not allowed further to infect and trouble this new colony.*

Fortunately, several factors worked in the Jews'

favor. Back in Amsterdam, Jewish businessmen had invested a great deal of money in the Dutch West India Company. The leaders of this important trading and colonizing organization therefore felt indebted to Jews everywhere. Furthermore, many Sephardic Jewish families ran international businesses and had a reputation of being successful colonists with money to spend. Since the Dutch authorities wanted the population in their new colony to grow, it would be irresponsible to turn away any potential settler.

Governor Stuyvesant was ordered to let the Jews in. But again, he protested:

To give liberty to the Jews will be very detrimental because the Christians cannot compete against them. Giving them liberty, we cannot refuse the Lutherans and the Papists.

21

By "Papists," he meant Roman Catholics, Rivka explained. Governor Stuyvesant was a member of the Dutch Reformed Church, which is a different sect of Christianity from Lutherans and Papists. Over the next couple of months, more letters were exchanged. "By the following spring," Rivka continued, "the Dutch West India Company forced Governor Stuyvesant to let us settle in Nieuw Amsterdam. Also during that time, Jews in Amsterdam answered our desperate pleas and sent us money to pay off Captain de la Motte. Finally, we were released from his clutches."

"So that's how we got to settle in Nieuw Amsterdam," Shoshana said, finally understanding "The Jews helped the Dutch West India Company, so they helped us."

"That's a good way to put it."

Feeling a sharp pang in her belly, Rivka kissed Shoshana on the cheek and left abruptly. It would be their last private time together in a long while. Later that evening, Rivka gave birth to her fifth child. She named him Abraham, after a beloved uncle in Holland. It was Uncle Abraham who had made sure the bosses of the Dutch West India Company knew that his family and their friends across the sea wanted to make their new home in North America.

CHAPTER THREE

ALONE IN THE WOODS

It was a difficult birth, and after it was over, Rivka was too weak to hold little Abraham. The midwife who attended the birth assured Rivka that she'd get her strength back soon. Abraham had an easier time of it. He was pink and wriggly and possessed an ear-splitting cry.

Shoshana pretended to be happy, but inside she was worried. It was frustrating enough having to share her mother's attention with three siblings. Now that there were four to compete with, Shoshana feared she might never again enjoy private time with her mother, or her father, for that matter. Perhaps it was time to focus on other things, like roses. Shoshana's twelfth birthday was fast approaching, and there was only one gift she wanted: a rose. A real, live rose that she could sniff and caress to her heart's content. When she shared her birthday wish with Christa, her friend said: "I hear there are roses growing wild in the woods."

"I find that hard to believe," Akiva said when Shoshana relayed the information. "I've been trapping animals in the woods almost since we arrived here eight years ago and never saw any roses." Akiva had become a trapper because Nieuw Amsterdam's climate was too cold to grow sugarcane, as he did in Brazil. Trapping was an easy business to start, and the money he made selling pelts from hare, beaver, and other small mammals supported his family and enabled him to employ the fathers of two more families.

"But Christa seemed so sure that roses are out there somewhere."

"It's probably just a rumor, but I suppose that anything is possible."

"I want to find out for sure, Pappa. May I pleeeease go into the woods and look for roses?"

Akiva pondered her request, then finally agreed. "Okay, Shoshana. Tomorrow before school, you can tag along with me. While I check my traps, you can check for roses."

Shoshana's brown eyes beamed with delight.

The next morning, while the rest of the family slept, Shoshana and her father crunched through last fall's leaves. They were guided by notches on trees Akiva had carved when he laid down his traps two days before.

A wide variety of trees, ferns, mosses, and other

plant life thrived in the woods, creating a canvas of every imaginable shade of green. Birds hidden in the dense foliage sang as if competing for best melody, loudest song, or longest note. One birdcall was so piercing that it reminded Shoshana of a shofar blast on Rosh Hashanah.

"It's nature's symphony," Akiva remarked. He had the heart of a poet, just like her mother, Shoshana thought admiringly.

"Do you remember what I taught you about marking your trail?"

"Yes, Pappa. At every fifth or sixth tree, cut a notch

in the bark pointing toward the direction we came from."

"Good. You should always remember to do this. It might save you from getting lost someday."

Within two hours, Akiva had sacked six hares and three beavers. Shoshana's quest for roses came up empty. Once she noticed a splash of color and ran up to it, but the flowers turned out to be orchids.

On their way home, Shoshana asked if she could try again the next day, but her father wasn't planning another trapping expedition for another week. His employees would take over while he met with Governor Stuyvesant and members of Shearith Israel, which was still pushing for permission to build its synagogue. These meetings, plus guard duty, plus helping his wife with the new baby, left Akiva Levy with precious little time for anything else.

Christa was also too busy to go rose hunting with Shoshana. In addition to homework, she was saddled with all the household chores while her father worked. Shoshana felt sorry for Christa because her parents, who used to argue all the time, were now separated. Christa lived with her father during the school year and spent summers with her mother, who lived almost fifty miles away in southern Nieuw Netherland. Christa missed her mother terribly when she was with her father, and vice versa. Shoshana felt fortunate that her own parents' relationship was so loving and strong.

Shoshana asked a few other friends to accompany

her on a rose hunt, but no one was interested. Shoshana was undaunted. If there really were roses in the forest, she wouldn't give up until she found them. So, the next morning after her father went to the fort but before her mother and siblings woke up, Shoshana borrowed her father's hunting knife, filled a wooden canteen with well water, and sneaked into the woods alone.

When Rivka woke up an hour later, she was instantly absorbed in caring for the baby and scolding the twins for bickering. It wasn't unusual for Shoshana to leave early for school, so Rivka wasn't overly concerned about her eldest child's absence.

Meanwhile, in the woods, Shoshana was notching tree number ten when a pair of large turkey vultures started fighting over a squirrel just a few feet away. Hissing and grunting, the birds of prey kicked up enough dirt, leaves, feathers, and fur to form a cloud big enough to engulf Shoshana. Before she could protect her face from the assault, a plume of dust flew into her eyes, causing intense pain.

Shoshana screamed.

Squeezing her eyes shut, she felt her way out of the cloud and used the hem of her skirt to rub the debris from her eyes. Finally, the cascade of tears subsided and her vision began to return, blurry at first. Blinking to regain focus, Shoshana saw a smudge in the distance that appeared to be glowing. At first, she thought her eyes were damaged and were seeing things that didn't exist. But as clarity returned, she saw a circular clearing bathed in sunlight beaming down through a hole in the canopy. In the middle of the clearing was a bush of some sort. Shoshana padded closer to investigate.

The bush came up to Shoshana's waist and spread out five feet in diameter. There were more than fifty buds and a single, partly open flower. Its inner petals were the color of ginger, the outer ones milky white with just a hint of orange. Shoshana bent down and dipped her nose into the blossom. When she inhaled, the fragrance was so deliciously sweet and strong that it made her scalp tingle and her arms break out in goose bumps.

"I wonder if…" Shoshana said out loud, impulsively grasping the stem.

"Ouch!" she yelped, snapping her hand back to her chest. When she looked down, she saw that her palm and fingers were starting to bleed. It was the happiest hurt she'd ever felt.

CHAPTER
FOUR

THE SECRET FRIEND

Reveling in her discovery, Shoshana examined every inch of the wild rosebush. She sniffed the lone blossom again and again until her nostrils grew too tired to notice the scent. She yearned to cut off the rose and take it home but hesitated, worrying that such an act might kill the bush. Yet, there were plenty of other buds ready to burst open, and one less flower probably wouldn't make a difference. Shoshana weighed the pros and cons carefully.

If nothing else, Shoshana needed evidence to show her father and anyone else who doubted that roses grew wild in the woods surrounding Nieuw Amsterdam. She plucked a large, thick leaf from a nearby beech tree and removed her father's hunting knife from its leather sheath. Using the leaf as a potholder to protect her hands from being pricked again, she cut the rose loose with a single swipe. To her delight, the flower remained robust, as if it was never removed from its source, and stayed that way the entire hour it took Shoshana to make her way home.

"Where on earth have you been?" said Rivka, who had just finished washing little Abraham's clothes.

"I went rose hunting, Mamma, and look what I found," Shoshana said, handing the rose to her mother.

"A rose! The color of ginger! I haven't seen one of these since I was a little girl in Amsterdam. Where did you find it?"

"Smell it, Mamma! What makes roses smell so good, anyway?" Shoshana replied, avoiding Rivka's question so that she wouldn't get into trouble.

"I have no idea, but what a relief from soiled diapers. Oh, Shoshana, this rose is as beautiful as you are. Now you know why I've always called you 'my beautiful rose.'

"Here, let's put it in a pot of water so it stays fresh," Rivka continued. "But on your way home from school today, why don't you ask Mr. Winchell to make you a pretty glass vase worthy of such a pretty flower?"

"That's a great idea, Mamma," Shoshana said, grateful that her mother apparently forgot to scold her about going into the woods alone.

"There are some coins on the kitchen shelf. Take what you need to pay Mr. Winchell."

After school, Shoshana and Christa ran to the glassblowing studio where Mr. Winchell and his apprentices worked. Glassblowing is a difficult skill

to master and quite fascinating to watch. It amazed
Shoshana that plain old sand, when heated, turned
into molten glass, the consistency of taffy that could be
stretched, twisted, blended, and molded like clay.

Most of Mr. Winchell's products were everyday
items such as cups, platters, and hurricane lamps.
Mr. Winchell was an artist at heart, however, so
he welcomed the opportunity to make something
decorative, like a bud vase.

"What color would you like it to be?" he asked
Shoshana.

"How about orange, like my flower?"

Mr. Winchell scattered a pile of red and yellow
glass chips on one end of a smooth table called a marver.
He grabbed his metal blowpipe, which was nearly as
long as his body. The molten glass sat in a ceramic pot,
which he called a crucible. The crucible was positioned

in an igloo-shaped brick furnace and heated to a very high temperature.

First, Mr. Winchell warmed the tip of his blowpipe. Next, he dipped it into the crucible to gather up a small quantity of glass. When the red-hot gather was the size of his fist, he carefully chilled the outside of the glob of glass to form a "skin," while the inner core remained hot. He blew a bubble into the glob, then dipped the tip of his blowpipe back into the crucible to gather up another small quantity of glass to cover the first.

Using gravity, air, and the marver, he carefully shaped the glob before reheating it in a "glory hole" located at the side of the furnace. Mr. Winchell then rolled the glowing orb back and forth along the colored chips until the glass glob was symmetrical.

He swung the pipe several times across his body to elongate the form and then blew another strong puff of air through the mouthpiece. This enlarged the bubble in the rapidly cooling glass. When the glass cooled enough to keep the bubble intact, he put the pipe back into the crucible to further increase the size of the gather. He repeated the puffing and gathering procedures until the orb and bubble were the size he was looking for.

Continuing to reheat the glass when necessary to keep it soft and pliable, Mr. Winchell used a dampened, folded newspaper and large tweezers called jacks to expertly pull and shape the material. At the same time, he rolled the pipe back and forth along the arms of his glass-blowing bench.

Once the glass was separated from the blowpipe, he transferred the object to another metal rod, attaching the base with a small dollop of molten glass. Next he and his assistants used shears and other tools to cut off the excess glass, open the top of the bud vase, and give it a delicate, wavy lip.

When he was satisfied with the piece, Mr. Winchell chilled the base with a special tool and knocked it off the pipe into his assistant's gloved hands. The last step was to place the vase in a lower-temperature oven, where it would remain overnight, cooling slowly so the vase wouldn't crack. When Shoshana returned the next day, the glass chips had melted into graceful spirals in various shades of orange. Tinier strings of red and yellow glass were peppered throughout, which made the finished piece even more beguiling.

Scattered on the floor were bits of excess glass that

had dripped off the gather each time it was removed from the crucible. To Shoshana, the glass droppings looked like jewels. She asked Mr. Winchell if she could have some.

"Of course," said Mr. Winchell, adding: "If you like those, you'll love this."

He slid open a drawer where he kept stacks of glass rods, each about 15 inches long. Through experimentation, Mr. Winchell had discovered that molten glass turned different colors when certain minerals were added. "Cobalt creates blue glass," he told Shoshana. "Iron rust makes green or brown glass. Sulfur compounds produce yellow glass; copper compounds turn the glass light blue or red. Tin turns glass white."

"Miraculous!" Shoshana gasped.

One by one, Mr. Winchell heated the tip of each rod until it got soft enough to drop off. Some he let drip into a pot of cold water; others dripped onto the marver. When they cooled, each glob looked like an oversized, tinted dewdrop. The drops that cooled in water sported a crackle finish but were as smooth to the touch as the air-cooled ones. No two looked exactly the same, and Shoshana thought they were all equally beautiful.

"They're called glass stones," Christa said. Her father had made her a set of them for a game called Mancala.

Shoshana paid Mr. Winchell for his materials, time, and talent, and she thanked him profusely for everything. Skipping home, Shoshana listened to the stones clinking together rhythmically in her pocket. It sounded like music, so she gave the noise a name: "Mr. Winchell's symphony."

Later that evening, Shoshana's mother sewed a light-brown rabbit pelt into a little pouch to store the glass treasures. Shoshana took the stones with her everywhere, including to the rosebush in the woods the following Friday morning. By then, the rose at home had wilted. It was her family's turn to host Shabbat dinner and worship services that evening. A rose perfuming the air would create such a festive atmosphere, her mother said. "Why don't you bring a fresh rose to Shabbat dinner every week?"

Using the trail she'd marked in the trees, Shoshana easily found her way back to the rosebush. By now, more than a dozen buds had opened. As she walked around the bush to decide which stem to cut, something strange caught her attention. There were *two* freshly cut stems: one from the rose she took the week before, and another on the opposite side of the bush. The second cut was smooth, as if made by a knife as opposed to the teeth of an animal. Someone else had been there. But who?

Shoshana looked around but didn't see anyone or hear anything, except the singing birds, some buzzing insects, and the *shhhhhhhhhh* of the hidden creek. Curious about her new discovery, but anxious to return home with a fresh new flower, Shoshana took a rose, using the potholder method she had invented the week before.

On her third visit, Shoshana found a total of four broken stems, two on her side of the bush and two on the other side. This time, before leaving with her rose, she placed five glass stones at the foot of the bush, one for each broken stem.

The following week, *six* blossoms were missing. The glass stones were gone, too. In their place, someone had left a little corncob doll. Shoshana looked around, then tentatively picked it up. The doll was wearing a leather dress with a black belt. It had black hair but no face. On its feet were moccasins, each with a tiny shell sewn on top. It was adorable.

Shoshana realized that the person who left the doll was probably as curious about her as she was about the stranger. She reached into her pouch and pulled out seven glass stones, arranging them at the base of the bush exactly where she had found the doll. Then she hid behind a tree and waited. And waited. And waited some more. When no one showed up, Shoshana grew bored and headed home. Next time, she'd visit the bush on Thursday instead of Friday. If her trading partner was as much a creature of habit as Shoshana was, perhaps they'd get there at the same time.

MEETING AT
THE BUSH

The following Thursday morning, the roses and
the stones were exactly the way Shoshana had left them.
She took her bloom, laid down a sixth stone, and waited
behind a large tree about 10 yards downwind from the
clearing. She played with the corncob doll to pass the time.

Before long, she heard several pairs of footsteps
in the leaves. Shoshana peeked around the tree and
saw a slender Indian girl about her age approaching
the bush, with two older women behind her. The girl's
black hair was woven into two neat braids that brushed
her waist. A string of wampum beads and freshwater
pearls encircled her neck. The girl's moccasins looked
as new and cared for as her dress. And what a dress! It
was made of leather, and on the front was an image of
beautiful ginger-colored rose with dark green leaves. As
the girl walked closer, Shoshana realized the rose was

actually a mosaic made of dyed porcupine quills cut to different lengths.

Shoshana's heart raced as she watched the stranger pick up the glass stones, admire them, and place them carefully into a pouch. In their place, the girl laid down not one, but two objects—a tiny wooden cradleboard and a three-pronged comb carved from deer antler. She took out a knife made of sharpened bone, stepped over to the beech tree, and cut off a couple of leaves, just as Shoshana had done.

Shoshana ducked behind her tree again, holding her breath to contain her exhilaration. She didn't want to frighten the stranger. Better to wait for an appropriate moment to reveal her presence, Shoshana thought.

Holding the leaves to protect her hand, the Indian girl used the blade to cut a single rose from the far side of the bush. The moment arrived. Shoshana stepped hesitantly into view and, in the sweetest, friendliest voice she could muster, said, "Hello."

The girl looked up and froze.

Maybe she doesn't understand Dutch, Shoshana thought. So she held up her pouch of stones and shook it. Next, she held up the corncob doll and smiled to signal her gratitude.

The stranger held up her leather pouch and shook it, too. Then they shook their pouches at the same time and started to giggle. Mr. Winchell's symphony had bridged the divide.

"My name is Shoshana."

"Sho-shay-na," the girl struggled to say. "I am called Ogee."

"Ogee. I like that name. Thank you for this doll, Ogee," Shoshana said.

"Thank—you—for—er..."

"...the glass stones?" Shoshana said slowly and clearly.

"That is how you say...?"

"Yes. They are very pretty, don't you think?

"Yes, very pretty. Pretty as flowers here."

Shoshana watched intently as Ogee picked up the cradleboard and demonstrated how to secure the doll to it. Next, Ogee picked up the comb and pantomimed how to use it. Shoshana took the comb and ran it once through her hair to indicate her understanding.

"Where are you from?" Ogee asked.

"That is a long story, but now I live in *Nieuw* Amsterdam."

"Are you Dutch?"

"No, I am a Jew."

"What is a Jew?"

"That is an even longer story, Ogee. Where are you from?"

"I live in a nearby village. My tribe is Lenape."

"Leh-NAH-pay?"

"Yes. Lenape means 'people.'"

"I speak Portuguese at home and Dutch at school. How did you learn to speak Dutch?"

"My father trades furs with the newcomers. He teaches Dutch words to me, but I have no chance to use them—until now."

Shoshana pointed to the rosebush. "Why do you take these flowers?"

"This plant is ogin, a gift from our Creator. My given name is Ogin, too. But my friends call me Ogee."

"Guess what! Shoshana means 'rose' in Hebrew. Hebrew is the language of the Jewish people."

"Rose. Much easier for me to say than Sho-shay-na."

"So, call me Rose. I like that. My mother calls me 'my beautiful rose.'"

Watching from a distance, Ogee's two aunts looked at each other and smiled.

Combining Dutch and sign language, Ogee told Shoshana that she had walked past the bush many times but never touched it because of the thorns. "Last week, when I saw the cut stem and bent beech leaves on the ground, I realized that I could take a flower without hurting my hand or killing the bush."

The bush's shrinking shadow reminded Shoshana that she was late for school. Although summer vacation was around the corner, she still had some final tests to take. "Ogee, I am sorry, but I must go now. Will you come here again, in seven days?"

"If you will be here, Rose," Ogee replied eagerly. She taught Shoshana to say *"la-peech knee-wëil,"* which means "I will see you again" in the Lenape language, and the new friends went their separate ways.

* * *

Shoshana stopped home briefly to put the rose in the vase before continuing on to school. She'd have to wait until after school to tell her parents all about Ogee and the gifts they had been trading.

On her way home, Shoshana stopped by Fort Amsterdam, where Akiva would be spending the night on guard duty.

"Pappa!" Shoshana yelled excitedly, giving him a big hug. "You'll never guess what happened to me today."

Akiva listened with fascination to Shoshana's meeting with the Lenape girl. He felt a brief pang of loss, realizing that Shoshana was becoming old enough to navigate her own way through the various paths that life would present her with; but this feeling was quickly replaced with the pride he felt in his daughter's ability to forge a friendship with a complete stranger…one who did not even speak her language!

"The Lenape are one of the friendliest and most helpful tribes we have encountered," Akiva told Shoshana. "When the earliest white people arrived in Nieuw Amsterdam, it was the Lenape who taught them better tracking and trapping techniques. This helped ensure that the colonists had enough to eat. As a matter of fact, I use some Lenape trapping techniques, myself. I'm really happy for you, Shoshana—the two of you will learn a lot from each other."

Shoshana was thrilled to learn of her father's connection to the Lenape and couldn't wait to share this new-found information with Ogee. She hugged her father good-bye and skipped home, now eager to share her adventure with her mother.

"She is a Lenape," Shoshana told her mother proudly.

Rivka's eyes flew wide open in terror. "She's an Indian?!" Rivka had never met an Indian and had only seen them occasionally from afar. But she knew of stories about violence between them and the European colonists, and her heart was immediately struck with fear. Still haunted by the pirates' attack of seven years ago, Rivka was weary of trusting anyone she did not know. To her, a stranger could mean danger.

"Shoshana, I'm not at all comfortable with you playing with an Indian girl. You know nothing about her. Indians live a completely different life than we do…it's best that you stay away from them." Turning to Bina and the twins, Rivka added: "That goes for all of you, too!"

Rivka's reaction stunned Shoshana.

"But Ogee is really nice."

"She may seem nice now, but she is just a child. She will learn her people's strange ways soon enough."

"Pappa said the Lenape are a friendly tribe and I believe him! Ogee and I even have the same name, sort of."

"The idea of a Hebrew name having anything in common with an Indian name is preposterous," Rivka barked. "How can you even communicate with her? Indians use sign language."

"That's not true, Mamma," Shoshana protested. "We spoke to each other. Ogee speaks a language called Lenape and she also learned some Dutch from her father, who has traded furs with the colonists."

"Is that so?" said Rivka. "Well, I hear that Indians trick people. Maybe the reason they trade with colonists is to spy on us. I don't want you seeing this girl again, Shoshana, and I am going to speak with your father about it as soon as he gets home." Shoshana's eyes welled with tears upon hearing her mother's last words. She ran to her room, threw herself down onto her bed and cried herself to sleep.

Rivka was too worried to sleep at all that night.

CHAPTER
SIX

THE LENAPE VILLAGE

The following day, Shoshana arrived home from school eager but anxious to hear about the decision her parents had made regarding her ability to see Ogee again. She found her father sitting in the living room, sifting through some papers in his hand, though he didn't seem to be reading them.

"Hi Pappa," she said, nervously trying to read his face. Akiva motioned her over and pulled up a chair so that they could be seated next to one another.

"Shoshana, your mother doesn't want you meeting with Ogee anymore," Akiva said in a low voice. "I am disappointed to learn that she feels this way, but not altogether surprised."

Shoshana felt her heart sink. "Why doesn't Mamma want me to be friends with the Indians?"

"You see, Shoshana, ever since we came to Nieuw Amsterdam, your mother has been very busy raising

47

you and your siblings and tending to all our household needs. On top of that, she helps hold our little Jewish community together by organizing Shabbat meals and holiday celebrations. She hasn't had time to meet our Lenape neighbors. To her, they are strangers, so she is suspicious of them."

"Just because they are strangers doesn't make them dangerous, though."

"Of course not. But it wasn't that long ago that we were attacked by the *piratas*. That incident changed your mother; it made her very fearful of strangers. She only wants to protect you from danger, be it real or imagined."

"Is anything she said about the Indians true?"

"It is true that certain Indian tribes have attacked the colonies or even declared war against colonists, usually because the colonists attacked them first and took their food and resources. But not all Indian groups are aggressive. In fact, each has a unique culture with their own set of beliefs, practices, and traditions. Individual Indians within the same group aren't necessarily the same, either, nor are the colonists. For example, Governor Stuyvesant and I couldn't be more unalike, yet we live in the same place and even have the same goal: to make this new land prosperous."

"Did you explain this to Mamma? Does she understand now? Does this mean I can see Ogee again?" Shoshana asked hopefully.

"I told your mother that I would come with you to your next meeting with Ogee, so that I could meet her myself and feel assured that you are safe."

"Oh, Pappa. Thank you so much!"

Akiva hugged Shoshana reassuringly, but what he did not share with his daughter was the fact that he and Rivka had just had their first real argument, and that it was about the Lenape. Rivka was not at all eased by Akiva's reassurances that the Lenape were a friendly tribe. She didn't want Shoshana wandering about the forest on her own and she didn't want Shoshana falling under the influence of a culture she knew nothing about. But Akiva was insistent that Shoshana's interaction with her new friend could be a positive experience—one he was curious to see unfold—and eventually Rivka begrudgingly deferred to her husband.

* * *

The next Thursday morning Akiva accompanied

49

Shoshana into the woods. When the girls met at their rosebush, he watched them as they hugged hello like long-lost sisters.

"Hello, Rose," Ogee said in Dutch.

"*Kwai*, Ogee," Shoshana said, using the Lenape word for "hi." Then she took Ogee's hand and walked her over to meet her father.

"Ogee, this is my father, Akiva Levy. He wanted to meet you, to see who I've been talking about all week!"

Ogee bowed her head toward Akiva. "Nice to meet you," she said, shyly.

Any questions or concerns Akiva may have had immediately vanished when he looked at Ogee. Her eyes told him everything he needed to know about her—they were warm and genuine and he understood why his daughter was so drawn to her new friend. He also observed that Ogee was accompanied by two older women, presumably there to ensure Ogee's safety.

"Ogee, it is a pleasure to meet you," Akiva said. "I have heard a lot about you—I'm so glad Shoshana has made a new friend."

Ogee smiled at Akiva and nodded her head in understanding.

"I think I can leave you two to play together now," Akiva said to Shoshana. "Mind the time, and don't come home too late. I will see you later."

Shoshana turned back to Ogee, excited to see her friend again and elated that the meeting between her new friend and her father had gone so smoothly. Then

Ogee handed Shoshana a beautiful gift - a deerskin dress with two ginger-colored roses on the front. Like Ogee's, this design was made of dyed porcupine quills.

"The women of my village took one of my dresses and put the design on it for you," Ogee said.

Shoshana held the dress up to her torso and smiled: "It's perfect! Thank you, Ogee! And please thank the women for me, too."

Ogee seemed equally overwhelmed by the gift Shoshana brought, a glass bud vase created by Mr. Winchell. The vase was similar to Shoshana's, but since every piece of blown glass is unique, there were subtle differences in the swirls and color patterns. Ogee held the vase to her heart—the girls' special sign of gratitude.

"How did you make this?" Ogee wondered. The Lenape were familiar with glass beads, which they acquired through trading. But Ogee didn't know other things could be made of glass.

51

"It was made by Mr. Winchell, the father of my friend, Christa. How he makes it is hard to describe. Someday, I'll take you to his workshop," Shoshana promised.

Ogee grabbed Shoshana's hand and tugged.

"Come. My parents invite you to see our home."

The notion of seeing a real Indian village enchanted Shoshana. She'd been curious about Ogee's parents and home life ever since they met. Summer vacation had just begun, and she'd woken up early to complete her chores before her meeting with Ogee.

"I'd love to," Shoshana replied.

The Lenape village wasn't far away, and Ogee knew her way around the woods as well as Shoshana knew her own bedroom. No marked trees were needed. Still, the trek took almost two hours because Ogee kept stopping to pick wild strawberries for the girls to nibble on, to point out medicinal plants, or to collect kindling, which Ogee carried in a holder strapped to her back.

Another detour took the girls to a patch of poisonous mushrooms sprouting from a rotting log. Ogee didn't know the Dutch word for "poisonous," so she scowled and waved her index finger over the fatal fungi.

"I understand," Shoshana said with a nod, correctly interpreting the warning.

When they finally arrived at their destination, Shoshana expected to see roads, square houses, and maybe a windmill or two, much like those in Nieuw

Amsterdam. Instead, she saw a sprawling campsite that seemed to be carved directly from nature. Nothing was

paved, and the dwellings and various worksites were situated along the natural contours of the countryside. Whoever had cleared the land to build their community apparently had left the most majestic trees standing.

A segment of the fast-flowing creek that Shoshana heard, but had never seen, wound through the Lenape village and fed a small lake nearby. Shoshana counted thirty round, windowless huts called wigwams. There was also a large longhouse used for community activities. Judging by the number of homes, campfires, and people milling about, Shoshana estimated that at least 500 people lived there.

"Welcome to the Lenape summer home!" Ogee said proudly.

The village comprised several dozen extended families, or clans, which inhabited this summer campsite from late spring through early autumn. At harvest time each year, the community moved their wigwams and most of their belongings to another campsite further inland to be closer to their crops.

The summer campsite was just a mile from the harbor, where Lenape fishermen used special nets woven from hemp to catch enough bounty to feed the entire community all summer long. In the woods, hunters used traps and bows and arrows to obtain all the meat, furs, antlers, and bones the community needed. Every part of the animal was used; nothing was wasted.

Ogee explained that clans were named to honor familiar animals, such as Turkey Clan, Raccoon Clan, Beaver Clan, and her own Turtle Clan. In addition to Ogee, her parents and six-year-old brother, the Turtle Clan included twenty-eight aunts, uncles, grandparents, great-aunts, great-uncles and first, second, and third cousins. Two children, a brother and sister orphaned when their parents died in a canoeing accident, also lived with the Turtle Clan.

Each family built its own wigwam by bending saplings into the proper shape and fastening them together with tree bark or animal skins cut into strips. Tied to the outside of the framework were woven cornstalks or pieces of bark that had been soaked in water and smoothed with stones. The floor of the wigwam was covered with animal skins, and people slept on stacks of evergreen boughs. Animal skins were also used to drape the doorways and keep out the wind.

The entire community worked together to build the longhouse. Its frame was made of wooden posts, poles, and saplings that were curved overhead to form the roof. The exterior was covered by bark and grass, which kept out the rain. Inside, the floors were covered with mats woven from the long, narrow leaves of cattail plants collected from nearby swamps.

Expert boat makers, the Lenape kept a dozen birch bark canoes at the eastern tip of the village. These strong, lightweight crafts were an important form of transportation. Lenape also traveled long distances by foot; their extensive network of trails was expanded by each generation.

At the western edge of the campsite were two sweat lodges, one for men and the other for women. Inside these huts, steam was created by heating rocks on a campfire then throwing cold water on them. If someone was ill, a special tea was served in the sweat lodge, or crushed herbs were added to the steam. The sweat lodges also had religious significance.

The Lenape believed in the "Great Manito," which means "all wise and good Creator." They also believed that every part of creation has its own spirit or "life." Because the Great Manito was present in all living creatures, the Lenape felt a strong relationship between themselves and the animals and plants that shared their world.

To honor the gifts provided by the Creator, Indians used special prayers or ceremonies for almost everything they did, from fashioning animal hides into clothing, to weaving turkey feathers into their headdresses, to catching fish, and kindling a fire. The Lenape used colorful face paints and performed elaborate dances to thank the animal spirits for nourishing their people and for providing both fur for warmth and bones for tools.

As Shoshana learned about the Lenape, she noticed similarities between their culture and her own. Although Jews believed that the world and everything in it was created by one God, "We also have special blessings to express our appreciation for food, clothing, health, rainbows, trees, our lives," Shoshana told her new friends as they sipped tea together.

Each Lenape contributed to their community, explained Ogee's mother, Sun Bird. In addition to healers and spiritual leaders, there were weavers, sewers, fishermen, trappers, toolmakers, potters, boat makers, carvers, berry gatherers, and cooks. There were painters, dancers, and makers of drums, flutes, and other musical instruments, too.

Almost everyone, including the children, got involved in farming. The Lenape's main crops were corn, kidney beans, and squash, collectively known as the "three sisters." During planting season, Ogee and her brother took turns sitting atop a raised platform in the middle of a cornfield to scare off blackbirds.

"That sounds like fun!" Shoshana said.

"Actually, it's boring," Ogee laughed.

Just outside the village, some teenage boys practiced using bows and arrows and throwing spears through rolling hoops. The younger boys competed in foot races, and little girls played with their dolls, helped the women grind corn, or just ran around and had fun.

Village elders were in charge of teaching skills and passing Lenape history and lore to the younger generations. The Lenape language was strictly oral. While having no written language had its disadvantages,

it did place an emphasis on storytelling to keep their people's history and traditions alive. As a result, children forged very strong, loving relationships with their grandparents.

Ogee's father, Soaring Hawk, was the Lenape's spiritual leader. He led many of the tribe's ceremonies and offered guidance to those who sought his counsel. He reminded Shoshana of her own father. Since Akiva knew the most about Jewish law and liturgy, he led services and advised congregants because Shearith Israel did not yet have a rabbi.

Sun Bird loved helping people, and had a talent for it, so she served as medicine woman. Her grandmother had taught her healing skills, which she was now teaching to Ogee. Sun Bird told Shoshana that over the generations, the Lenape discovered many plants that had the power to relieve pain, soothe rashes, or cure disease. Rainwater that collected in tree stumps or rocks was also thought to have healing powers.

In the Lenape's longhouse, Sun Bird maintained neat rows of small clay pots, each containing a different type of herb, root, tree bark, or other remedy, such as skunk oil and roasted onion syrup for colds or mud to treat burns. She also kept a hollowed-out deer antler within easy reach.

"What is that for?" asked Shoshana.

"If someone is bitten by a poisonous snake, we use it to suck out the venom," Sun Bird explained, as Ogee's father translated.

"Brilliant," Shoshana said. She recounted the story of a young boy she knew from school who had been bitten by a pit viper and almost died.

She found her conversation with Soaring Hawk equally illuminating. He showed her a sacred wooden statue called Manito Kan, which represented the Great Spirit.

"Do you pray to the statue?" Shoshana asked.

"No, it is a symbol."

"In Judaism, we call our Creator 'God' or 'Hashem.' We learn God's wisdom through a special book called the Torah," Shoshana explained.

"Everyone should worship as they see fit," Soaring Hawk said, smiling. "The Earth is big enough for all beliefs."

That's exactly what my father would say, Shoshana thought.

CHAPTER
SEVEN

TROUBLE IN THE LEVY HOME

Back at the Levy home, Shoshana's parents argued once again.

"Why are you encouraging her to meet that girl? Parents are supposed to support each other." Rivka said to Akiva in a voice laced with anger and disappointment.

"I can't support what you say when it's unfounded and teaches our children the wrong lesson, Rivka," Akiva responded, trying to stay calm. "I met Ogee and I have no concerns. Why are you so afraid of the Lenape, anyway?"

"They're completely different from us. What if they try to convert Shoshana to their religion?"

"I have traded with a number of Lenape, and they have never pushed their beliefs onto me. In fact, I've never even heard them talk about their religion to outsiders. They seem quite private in that regard."

"If Shoshana spends too much time with them, they won't be able to keep it private. We need to protect her, Akiva."

"Rivka, every Shabbat, who lights the candles and says the blessing with you?"

"As the oldest daughter, Shoshana does."

"On Passover, who helps you prepare the Seders?"

"Shoshana does, of course."

"Do you think we do a good job teaching our children about Jewish wisdom and history?"

"Yes."

"Then, what makes you think Shoshana would be so quick to abandon her heritage?"

"I'm...I'm not sure. We never discussed it."

"Maybe it's time to have that discussion."

"Perhaps. Although I still think you should support me when I tell Shoshana what she can and cannot do. How can she respect what I say if her father disagrees with me? Awakened from their naps by their parents raised voices, the twins called out for their mother and Abraham began wailing. Rivka ran to them, slamming their bedroom door behind her.

Shoshana heard their argument, too, from the other side of the front door. She had just returned from Ogee's village and was disappointed to learn that her father had not been able to change her mother's mind. She was even wearing her new rose dress, which she was eager to show off. After realizing that her parents were deadlocked, she ran back into the woods, put on

her regular clothes, and buried the dress under some leaves next to a big oak tree. She cut a small notch at the bottom of the tree so she'd remember it where it was.

Shoshana brushed the dirt off her hands and knees and proceeded home. Her mother was still in the back room. Her father was sitting at the kitchen table, looking tired and anxious.

"Do you think Mamma will *ever* change her mind about the Lenape?" Shoshana asked.

"Yes, sweetheart. But she'll need more time. We must be patient."

Rivka walked into the kitchen, the twins in tow. She managed a tight smile for her daughter but could not bring herself to ask about Shoshana's day with the Indian girl.

"It's getting late. There's some leftover stew. Please eat it, then it's time for bed."

"Yes, Mamma."

Akiva said nothing as he rose up from his chair. With a heavy sigh, he left the house and headed to the fort to offer an extra night of guard duty.

As she lay in bed, Shoshana began thinking about her friend, Christa Winchell. When Mr. and Mrs. Winchell separated, Christa felt as though her world collapsed. Christa had tried every argument she could think of to bring her parents back together until realizing that the situation was hopeless. Although the Winchells assured their daughter that the breakup was not her fault, Christa still felt somewhat responsible.

Shoshana had tried to comfort Christa, but nothing seemed to help. Christa had been depressed for months. She cried over the smallest things, like putting too much yeast in the bread dough or forgetting to do her homework. The first year of the separation, Christa almost flunked out of school. Now three years later, she was finally getting comfortable living with one parent at a time and her grades were back to normal.

As she thought about Christa, Shoshana stared at the rafters above her bed. Her eyes followed the grains whirling across the wood and she felt as confused and unsettled as the pattern above her appeared to be. *What if Mamma and Pappa split up, too?* she thought. *And what if it's all my fault?*

Chapter Eight

Bittersweet Goodbyes

Shoshana continued visiting Ogee. Though she felt guilt-ridden over the trouble it was causing at home, she was grateful for the escape it provided her. Before their disagreement over the Lenape surfaced, Akiva and Rivka had rarely squabbled over anything. In fact, their conversations were normally filled with affection, not tension. Now, arguments over Shoshana and Ogee boiled up almost every time the Levys spoke to each other. The summer dragged on with no compromise in sight. Part of Shoshana wished to cut off contact with Ogee if it would make her parents stop fighting. But a far bigger part of her desperately needed Ogee's friendship, now more than ever.

Shoshana always felt better after talking about her problems. Keeping her troubles inside made her feel like a bubble that could burst at any minute. But

who could she talk to now? She didn't dare express
her mixed-up feelings to her mother, and all her father
could say was, "Be patient." If Shoshana talked to a
neighbor or her teacher, it might feed the same rumor
mill that helped form Rivka's negative opinion of
Indians.

When Shoshana told Christa that she was afraid her
parents' marriage was crumbling, it made both girls feel
worse.

"It used to be like that in my house," Christa
admitted. "Eventually my parents decided they'd be
happier living apart. I only wish they had considered
my happiness too."

It seemed ironic that Ogee was the only person
who could make Shoshana feel better. Each week at the
rosebush or the Lenape camp, Ogee always found ways
to cheer up Shoshana. Sometimes, she'd suggest a game
to play, which took Shoshana's mind off her troubles.
Usually, though, Ogee merely listened as Shoshana
vented her feelings. When Ogee did speak, she never
offered advice. Instead, she'd share wisdom from the
Lenape elders, such as: "When two people are married
for a long time, their love is protected deep within their
hearts."

Ogee's reassurance became a salve on Shoshana's
soul.

Ogee's Dutch was improving markedly, and
Shoshana was picking up some more Lenape words. By

the end of the summer, the girls had created their own private language, a blending of Dutch, Lenape, and sign language. Whenever they parted ways, they'd jiggle their sacks of glass stones. On the last day of summer, Shoshana dug up her rose dress, knock off the dirt, and hid it under her bed. She hoped for an opportunity to wear it again before she grew out of it.

Green leaves of summer giving way to brilliant gold, orange, and red usually filled Shoshana with delight. This year, however, the approach of autumn filled Shoshana with dread. It was almost harvest time, and the Lenape were preparing to move to back to their winter haven. Ogee and Shoshana met at the rosebush as usual, but this time, it was to say good-bye. Was it good-bye until next spring, or good-bye forever? Neither knew for sure. The Lenape's winter campsite was at least a six-hour walk from the rosebush. And that was without snow on the ground.

Akiva was also dreading the change of seasons, but for him this was nothing new. Each year, with luck before the first snowfall, he carried out one final round of trapping that lasted four days and four nights. During these sojourns, he'd camp alone in the forest, which was almost unbearable to a man who thrived on social interaction. His only consolation this year would be a break from the near-constant bickering with Rivka. Perhaps being apart for a few days would give them both some perspective and help them rekindle the love he knew they still had for each other.

When Rivka found out that the Lenape were moving far away, she was relieved. She could tell that Shoshana was sad about losing her friend and she wanted to comfort her; but a wall had developed between her and her daughter because the one topic Shoshana wanted to discuss was the one Rivka found most disdainful. When they spoke now, it was usually about what to wear or chores, but little more.

What Shoshana missed most were her mother's wonderful bedtime stories. Whether they were real or made up, those stories had been the glue that bonded them together. Instead, Shoshana played with her glass stones every night before bed, grouping and regrouping them according to size and according to color. She loved their coolness, their smoothness, their sheen, the noise they made when she clinked them together, and especially all the good memories they held. Still, she would trade her last glass stone if it would make her parents happy again.

Like her father, Shoshana needed a break from home life. So, when Akiva invited her to accompany him on his year-end trapping excursion, Shoshana couldn't pack her bag fast enough.

"I'll write a note to your teacher excusing you from school," Akiva said. "But you'll need to make up all the work you miss."

"I promise, Pappa."

CHAPTER NINE

THE SLIPPERY SLOPE

The first day of trapping was perfect. Akiva set eighteen traps over a two-mile radius. There was enough time to visit the rosebush, as well. Shoshana gave her father the grand tour. "This is where I found the corncob doll! And this is the tree I hid behind the first time I met Ogee!" Shoshana said excitedly, hopping from place to place. "I have an idea, Pappa. Let's go to the Lenape summer camp. There's so much to show you."

"Nobody will be there, though."

"I know, but the longhouse will be standing. I'm sure it would be okay if we slept there, just one night."

"I suppose that would be all right. But we must leave the longhouse exactly as we found it."

"Of course, Pappa."

It felt strange to Shoshana, walking up the ridge to the campsite without Ogee by her side. But her father was there, and she couldn't wait to show him the looms, the place where the Lenape danced and beat their drums, the sweat lodges, the rack where herbs were dried, the canoe yard. It would be like reliving the best summer of her life.

Akiva was surprised by the size of the campgounds and the obvious sophistication of the Lenape lifestyle. He was especially impressed by a rack the tribe constructed to stretch their animal skins.

"Where are the wigwams you told me about?" Akiva asked as they made their way to the longhouse.

"Ogee told me they get folded up and taken to the winter camp," Shoshana said.

Once inside the longhouse, Akiva complimented the structure's sturdy construction and cozy interior. He and Shoshana slept like bear cubs in their den. The next morning, they rolled up their sleeping bags and sealed up the entrance of the longhouse tightly before leaving.

Akiva decided to use the opportunity to lay some traps on the far side of the settlement. He wasn't familiar with this terrain, however, which was far rougher than what he was used to. But the weather seemed to be holding, and he figured there'd be more animals around to capture since Nieuw Amsterdam trappers normally didn't venture out so far. Father and daughter would spend a second night in the longhouse then collect their bounty the next morning before doubling back to retrieve animals from traps they had laid the first day. That was the plan, at least.

Shoshana and Akiva were two miles beyond the Lenape summer camp when nature struck with a vengeance—a sleet storm. With great difficulty, Shoshana helped her father rig a lean-to. That provided some shelter as the clouds hurled freezing needles that turned the ground into a half-frozen, muddy mess. When the precipitation let up some two hours later, Akiva had a change of heart.

"Shoshana, let's head home today instead of tomorrow. We'll grab as many traps as possible on the way and forget about those we can't find readily." Shoshana agreed wholeheartedly. They held hands as they searched for the cuts they had made in the trees to guide them. To Akiva's utter dismay, all the traps were empty—all except one, which managed to slide to the bottom of a ravine during the storm.

Releasing her father's hand, Shoshana inched her way to the edge of the small chasm.

"Look, Pappa, there's a fox in that trap!" Shoshana said, bending forward slightly get a better view.

71

"Be careful, Shoshana!" Akiva shouted.

The sight of the trapped fox made Akiva's heart rate quicken. Red fox pelts were worth a small fortune, but this was an even rarer catch: a silver fox, and an especially large specimen, at that.

Shoshana grabbed onto a sapling to anchor herself as she leaned over a bit farther. The ravine was a good fifteen feet deep, with steep, slick walls of ice, mud, rock, and exposed roots. "Poor fox," she whispered.

Akiva joined Shoshana to evaluate the situation. His family could certainly use the money that fox pelt would fetch. On the other hand, the retrieval process would be terribly tricky. It would require delicate footwork and plenty of muscle to lower himself to the bottom of the ravine, release the fox from the trap, secure the carcass to his belt, and climb back up the slippery slope without the benefit of a rope. Some of the rocks and roots jutting out of the walls could be used as handholds and footholds, but even so, there was no way to accomplish the mission without getting completely covered in mud.

After several long minutes of weighing the benefits of selling the animal against the risk of recovering it, he concluded: "I think we should let this one go."

"Okay, Pappa," Shoshana said, still leaning over.

Suddenly, a small object fell out of her coat and cascaded to the bottom of the ravine and into a puddle right next to the dead fox.

"Oh, no!" Shoshana yelped. "My glass stones!"

"Stay calm," said Akiva.

Suddenly, Akiva found himself weighing whether to risk venturing into the ravine. Shoshana assured him that Mr. Winchell could replace the stones, as much as she loved the original batch. However, the two prizes down there had already given Akiva the excuse he needed to make the attempt.

"Don't worry, Shoshana, I'll get your stones."

"It looks so slippery, Pappa. Please be careful."

"Of course I'll be careful. Grab onto that sapling again, Shoshana, and give me your other hand."

Shoshana held onto the baby tree as tightly as she could. Her father lay down on his stomach and began to lower himself slowly. When he reached the point at where he had to let go of Shoshana's hand, he was still a good ten feet from the bottom. He grabbed onto one root, then another, digging his feet into the frosty mud, step by step. But his hands quickly grew numb, which made him lose his grip and start sliding downward uncontrollably. He might have slid safely to the bottom, but his right foot was caught by a root that elbowed out of the earthen wall like a stirrup. The top half of his body flipped over backward. His ankle cracked with a loud, sickening sound.

"Aaargh!" Akiva screamed, pain searing his ankle and lower leg like a red-hot branding iron.

Shoshana gasped in horror at the sight of her father, helpless and in agony, hanging upside down, his right foot twisted into an unnatural position and pinned to the wall by that stubborn root. His waved his hands around, trying to feel for something to grab onto. His head hovered just inches from the floor of the ravine.

"Hold on, Pappa. I'm coming!" Shoshana screamed, frantically searching for a means of lowering herself to his side.

"No, Shoshana, don't!" Akiva cried out between groans. "You'll get hurt! Go find help! Quickly!"

"All right," Shoshana said, although she had no idea which way to run. Then she looked over her shoulder and spied a large boulder whose silhouette reminded her of a horse's head. She recognized it from Ogee's description of the landmarks on the way to the Lenape's

wintering ground. Hope rippled through Shoshana's body. *They must be nearby!*

She darted past Horse Head Rock and kept on running. She followed a series of cairns—piles of rocks used to mark the trail to the Indians' winter home—that Ogee once described. Before long, Shoshana saw the familiar gray smoke drifting up from the Lenape campfires. She ran toward the campsite as fast as she could, screaming, "Help me! Help me!" in Lenape. No one at the camp could hear her, but someone in the group noticed movement in his peripheral vision, looked up, and alerted the others. Ogee and her parents dropped what they were doing and raced toward her.

"Rose! Rose!" Ogee squealed with delight, running toward Shoshana. "What are you doing here?!" But the moment Ogee saw Shoshana's face up close, she realized something was terribly wrong.

Breathlessly, Shoshana used their special language to explain what happened to her father. Ogee translated for the adults, who immediately organized a rescue operation. Ogee's father, Soaring Hawk, sprinted back to the Turtle Clan's wigwam and emerged with a coiled rope and a stone ax. Her mother ran home, too, to grab her kit of medicinal herbs and a stack of softened bark. Three men from other clans—Oray, Neka, and Ahanu—volunteered to join them. They contributed a stack of long, straight branches and a sturdy sled, which was attached to two long pulling poles. Soaring Hawk and

Shoshana quickly stuffed backpacks with other items that might be needed.

The group jogged through the woods, with Shoshana leading the way and Ogee running right behind her so she could continue translating details of Akiva's ordeal. When they finally arrived at the ravine, Akiva's situation was unchanged, except that now he was only semi-conscious. Shoshana's fear grew upon seeing her father again, still hanging upside down but now looking lifeless. She clutched Ogee's arm.

"Mr. Levy, can you hear me?" Ogee called out in Dutch.

"Wha, who is there?" Akiva said weakly.

"It is me, Ogee."

"Sho-sha…Sho-sha…"

"Do not worry, Mr. Levy. Sho-shay-na is here, too. So are my parents and other grownups. We will help you now."

"Everything's going to be okay, Pappa," Shoshana said over and over. "Be strong! I love you!"

Sun Bird instructed the girls to keep talking to Akiva so he'd stay alert. Meanwhile, Soaring Hawk deftly tied a rope around his waist and handed the other end to Neka and Oray, who were both tall and extremely muscular. They held the rope tightly as Soaring Hawk rappelled down the wall, pausing where Akiva's foot was caught in the root. At the same time, Ahanu used his enormous strength and agility to ease himself to the bottom of the ravine. Once there, he got down on all fours and maneuvered himself beneath Akiva so he could support the injured man's head, shoulders, and upper back. This took pressure off Akiva's broken ankle, allowing Soaring Hawk to safely cut the root and release Akiva's foot. Soaring Hawk leapt down to join Ahanu, who was already on his feet, helping Akiva into a sitting position.

With Ogee's and Shoshana's help, Sun Bird handed down the sled. Akiva was gently laid on the sled and secured with the rope. Slowly but steadily, Soaring Hawk and his comrades used ropes and muscle power to carefully raise Akiva safely out of the ravine. Sun Bird laid a blanket on her patient's chest and arms to keep him warm and prevent him from going into shock. Using strips of cloth and a length of tree bark as a splint, she wrapped his broken ankle tightly. Then she used small tree limbs and more cloth to immobilize his right leg from thigh to foot.

As she worked, Shoshana and Ogee started a small fire, boiled some water, and made a batch of willow-bark tea.

"Here, sip some of this," Sun Bird told Akiva. This time, it was Shoshana who served as translator. "It should ease your pain."

"Thank you," Akiva whispered. "Thank you all. I am humbled by your bravery and your kindness."

Soaring Hawk looked up at the clouds and shook

his head slowly. "The Sky is preparing to send us snow," he predicted. "We cannot risk taking Akiva back to the Lenape camp. If we do, the snow will be too deep to bring him home anytime soon. We must take him directly to his wife."

Shoshana was jubilant to hear this plan. She couldn't fathom dragging her father back to Nieuw Amsterdam by herself. But then she thought about her mother, and her jubilation changed to worry. To Rivka Levy, Indians were savages, not saviors. All sorts of uncomfortable scenarios formed in Shoshana's mind.

How would Mamma react to the sight of six Lenape pulling her badly injured, snow-covered husband home in a sled? Would she blame the Indians for Pappa's injury and slam the door in their faces? How would Ogee's parents react? Would they forbid Ogee from being friends with me? And what if Mamma called the militia before I had a chance to explain what the Lenape did for Pappa? What if soldiers came and arrested Soaring Hawk and the others, or worse, shot them on sight?

CHAPTER
TEN

A HOMECOMING TO REMEMBER

The snow fell lightly at first, then collected into large, foreboding flakes that clumped together before settling to earth. The rapid accumulation turned walking into a chore, especially for the men who were pulling Akiva in the sled. When the snow got too deep, the Lenape took out snowshoes and lashed them to their moccasins. They had an extra pair for Shoshana.

The girls spent a large part of the five-hour hike back to Nieuw Amsterdam discussing ways to prevent Rivka from becoming scared or upset. When Shoshana's house finally came into view, Ogee shared their plan with the others so that everyone would know exactly what to do.

First, the Lenape slid Akiva to the foot of the porch steps and released him from the sled. Soaring Hawk and Sun Bird helped him up and supported him as the others hid behind trees. Shoshana quietly entered the house alone and closed the door gently but quickly behind her.

Rivka and the children were gathered around a roaring fire in the hearth. Baby Abraham was propped in his high chair. Rivka was feeding him with one hand and stirring a large pot of stew with the other. The house was warm as summer, and the delicious smell of stew made Shoshana's mouth water. She didn't realize how hungry she was. Rivka was facing in the opposite direction and didn't realize anyone had come in.

"Mamma?" Shoshana said sweetly, brushing the snow off her head and shoulders.

"Shoshana! I didn't expect you home until tomorrow. Where's your father?"

"I have bad news and good news."

"Bad news and good news?"

"Well, the bad news is that Pappa broke his ankle."

"Oh dear!"

"The good news is that some very nice people put his ankle in a splint and carried him home for me. They're waiting with him right now, just outside our front door. Mamma, I don't know what I would have done without their help. I told them all about you, and they can't wait to meet you and the rest of the family."

"How wonderful, Shoshana. Please, invite your friends in from this frigid weather. Perhaps they can join us for dinner. You must be famished."

Smiling, Shoshana opened the door, stuck out her arm and waved. Soaring Hawk and Snow Bird helped

Akiva up the stairs and over the threshold. Ogee and the others filed in, as well.

Rivka dropped her stirring spoon into the pot and involuntarily took two steps backward. She couldn't believe her eyes. Here was her husband standing on one foot, his right leg wrapped beyond recognition, and he was surrounded by Indians, of all people! They were laughing and chattering in two languages—three, if you counted sign language. What on earth was going on here?

Shoshana linked arms with Ogee. "Mamma, this is Ogee, the friend I told you about."

"Pleased to finally meet you," Ogee said shyly, using her finest Dutch.

Shoshana presented Soaring Hawk and Sun Bird. "And these are Ogee's parents."

"*Kwai*," the couple said in unison, smiling broadly.

"Rivka," Akiva said before his wife could utter a word, "if these good people didn't come to my rescue at Shoshana's bidding, I might be dead right now, and Shoshana might be stranded in the woods."

Finally, Rivka's shocked, frightened expression began to disappear. She hugged Shoshana then walked over to Akiva and threw her hands around his neck. "I'm sorry, Akiva…for everything," she whispered in his ear.

As she slowly stepped back, Rivka made eye contact with each Lenape Indian, one by one. Then she looked down at the floor.

"I...I don't know what to say," Rivka said, choking back tears as Ogee translated, "... except thank you."

Rivka helped lower Akiva into the only upholstered chair in the house. Responding to Snow Bird's gestures, Shoshana pulled a wooden stool up to the chair and gently placed Akiva's injured foot on top. With Ogee continuing to translate, Sun Bird instructed Rivka to keep the injured ankle elevated as much as possible. She also recommended that Akiva pack his ankle in snow several times a day to reduce the swelling. After two days, he was to switch to warm-water soaks.

Next, the medicine woman handed Rivka a pouch filled with willow bark shavings. "Brew this into a tea and give him two or three cups twice a day until the

pain subsides. There should be enough left over to treat a headache or any pain in the body."

"Thank you so much," Rivka said, awed by this strong, statuesque woman who radiated so much warmth.

Oray handed Akiva a cane fashioned from a sturdy branch, and Sun Bird demonstrated its use.

"I almost forgot," said Soaring Hawk. He gave Shoshana her pouch of glass stones, which he'd managed to grab during the rescue. Shoshana said "thank you" in Lenape, and clutched them to her heart. Ogee took out her pack of stones, too. The girls shook their respective pouches and said in unison, "Mr. Winchell's symphony!" Everyone laughed.

Then Oray said something in Lenape and left. He returned a moment later with a burlap sack. Inside was the frozen fox carcass, still stuck in the trap.

"I forgot all about that!" Akiva said, delighted by this surprise.

Rivka listened to everyone explain about her husband's accident, Shoshana's bravery, and the cooperation needed to mount such a daring rescue. The love and the kindness engulfing her family at that moment made Rivka feel as though the Almighty was in the room, blessing her, blessing them all. She bent down and kissed Akiva's forehead.

"I owe you, Shoshana, and all your Lenape friends a profound apology," she whispered to her daughter.

"It's all right, Mamma," Shoshana interrupted. "You were only trying to protect…"

"No, my sweet rose, I must say this." Rivka looked at Ogee and her parents. "Instead of getting to know you as individuals, I prejudged you based on false rumors. I was prejudiced against all Indians, just like Governor Stuyvesant was prejudiced against all Jews when we first arrived in Nieuw Amsterdam. I can't believe I behaved so badly."

"Let's forget the past and get to know each other now so we can have a better future," Soaring Hawk suggested in Dutch. Over dinner and through the rest of the night, the Levys and the Lenape did just that. It wasn't always easy to communicate, but they worked hard to share their ideas, customs, and history.

Among other things, the Levys were surprised to learn how wild and wooded Nieuw Amsterdam was before the newcomers arrived. Many plants that the Levys never heard of, or thought were poisonous, were actually edible, such as crabapples and huckleberries. Rivka was thrilled to learn that cattail fluff could be used to diaper a baby. Currently, Abraham's diapers were cut from old blankets, which had to be washed out every day. It was Rivka's least favorite chore.

Soaring Hawk's description of drawing sap from maple trees, and turning the sap into sugar, gave Akiva an idea for a new business. "In Brazil, I used to grow sugarcane," he said. "I didn't realize there was a source of sugar in our new country, too."

For their part, the Lenape found their imaginations stirred by Akiva's description of a faraway place called

Brazil and an even farther away place called Israel, where the Jewish people originated.

"If Israel is the Jewish people's Promised Land, how did Jews come to live in Brazil?" Ogee asked.

Akiva explained that the Jews had been expelled from the Promised Land more than 2,000 years ago and from many other places since. Ogee and her family were horrified. "Why were they forced to leave?" she asked.

"The reasons varied," Akiva said. "In some cases, the Jewish community grew so large that it was seen as a threat to those in power. In other cases, Jews were punished because they didn't accept the beliefs held by the majority population.

"In Spain, beginning in the 1300s, Jews were targeted mostly because they were wealthy."

"I do not understand," Soaring Hawk interjected.

"You see, the Spanish throne was financed by the Jews and felt indebted to them," Akiva explained. "By

stripping Jews of their wealth and killing them or kicking them out, the Inquisition removed any power or influence Jews might otherwise have over Spain's rulers.

"The Inquisition was a court formed by the Catholic Church in the 1300s and 1400s that forced Jews to convert to Catholicism. Those who refused to convert were either expelled or killed."

"How awful!" said Snow Bird.

Shoshana noted that her grandparents, along with other Jews who managed to flee Spain, found new homes in tolerant countries, such as Holland, also known as the Netherlands, and later, in Dutch colonies, such as Recife, Brazil, where the Levys used to live.

Although Rivka and Akiva Levy didn't move to Brazil until 1635, Jewish families had been living there since the early 1500s, but under constant threat of being arrested and sent back to Spain and the Inquisition. Only when the Dutch took over Brazil in 1624 were the Jews permitted to worship freely.

"Then what happened?" Ogee asked.

"The Jewish population flourished. We worked as religious school teachers, scientists, writers, and poets. We collected taxes, lent money, exported sugar, and did lots of other things. Before long, more than half of all the major plantations in Recife were owned by Jews. In 1636, we opened the New World's first synagogue. It was called Kahal Tzur Israel—Congregation of the Rock of Israel.

"But eventually the Spanish Inquisition spread to

Portugal, and our period of freedom abruptly ended. When the Portuguese recaptured Recife in 1654, the Jews were ordered to leave," Akiva recounted. "We took what we could and sailed away, leaving our beloved homes and synagogue, as well as our businesses and our dreams behind."

Rivka burst into tears and ran out of the room. Akiva grabbed his cane and hobbled into their bedroom behind her.

"I'm sorry, Rivka. I didn't mean to upset you by dredging up the past."

"No, Akiva. It isn't that."

"What's wrong, then?"

"I used to feel superior to the Indians, just like the Catholics felt superior to the Jews. They treated Jews as sub humans; they even called us pigs."

"Yes, Rivka. It pains me to remember this, too."

"I called the Indians 'savages' even though they never did anything to hurt us. I judged out of ignorance and fear. I'm no better than the court of the Inquisition."

"Rivka, it may be true that you were prejudiced. But you never tried to convert Indians like the Catholic Church tried to convert us. And you certainly never killed anyone for disagreeing with you."

"Oh, Akiva, I could *never* do anything like that," Rivka said between sobs.

"Of course not. So, now that you've had a chance to meet some of our Lenape neighbors, what do you think of them?"

"They are not savages at all. On the contrary, they are kind and caring. They seem to treat everyone like family, including strangers. Look what they did for you, Akiva, saving your life and making sure you and Shoshana got home safely. This is how Jews would be expected to act, as we are reminded each Passover."

"You're so right, Rivka. One of the messages of Passover is to be kind to strangers. Before Moses led our people to the Promised Land, we were strangers in Egypt."

"We should tell the Lenape about Passover."

"Yes, we should. Come to think of it, there's another Jewish holiday coming up sooner that the Lenape might appreciate."

Rivka thought for a moment and then smiled in agreement with Akiva.

CHAPTER ELEVEN

THE NEW YEAR OF TREES

Two months later, Rivka's face glowed with delight as she welcomed Ogee and her family back to the Levy home. It was almost sundown. Tu B'Shvat, the Jewish New Year of Trees, was about to begin.

"We're so happy to see you again," said Rivka. She thanked Snow Bird for the nuts and dried fruit she brought for the celebratory meal. Soaring Hawk brought a bundle of cattail fluff for Abraham's diapers and toys for the other Levy children. Ogee brought some extra kindling for the hearth. As planned, Shoshana and Ogee both wore their rose dresses.

Akiva presented Snow Bird with a pelt he'd made from the silver fox that had fallen into the ravine. The pelt—black frosted with white—was unusually soft and subtle, owing to the special effort he put into preparing it. "Please accept this token of my gratitude for saving my life," Akiva said. "It's the least I could do."

"I have something for you, Ogee," said Shoshana. She handed her friend a delicate, ginger-colored glass rose on a green stalk. The stalk had small white bumps to represent thorns, but they weren't sharp. It was made by Mr. Winchell.

"It looks like our flower!" Ogee exclaimed, while her parents ooohed and ahhhed. "Thank you, Rose. I will love this forever!"

Soaring Hawk complimented Akiva on the speed at which his ankle was healing. "You followed Snow Bird's advice, I see," he said with a chuckle. Akiva nodded and wiggled his foot. He no longer needed the cane, although he still walked with a limp.

Snow Bird, who had learned a little Dutch, said, "Can you tell us what Tu B'Shvat means?"

Rivka explained that the holiday of Tu B'Shvat is named for the date it falls on, the fifteenth of the Hebrew month of Shvat. "In ancient Israel, Tu B'Shvat was the cut-off date for collecting taxes on fruit trees."

"Taxes on fruit trees?" Ogee asked.

"In ancient times, the Jewish people tithed one-tenth of their harvest to support the sacred work of the temples and to help the poor," Rivka said. "We still try to do this today. Jews believe that each one of us plays a role in building a greater society. So, if you own a fruit tree or another form of wealth, it is your responsibility to share that wealth with those less fortunate than you. Judging by your actions, it's clear that this is a value the Lenape share."

"Yes, but we don't believe that anyone can 'own' a tree or the land," Soaring Hawk countered. "These belong to the Great Manito, the Great Spirit. We are only inhabitants borrowing these gifts to survive, and taking care of them so our children and our children's children can enjoy them after we are gone."

"I understand," Rivka said, "Even so, you shared something else of value, your strong bodies and clever minds, to save my husband's life when he couldn't save himself. To me, that is an extraordinary way to tithe."

Soaring Hawk and Snow Bird looked at each other and nodded.

Appearing confused, Ogee asked, "If harvest time is in the fall, why is Tu B'Shvat celebrated in winter?"

"Because this date is considered the official end of last year's harvest season and the beginning of this year's planting season," Akiva said. "In addition to tithing, Tu B'Shvat teaches us to appreciate and honor the cycle of the seasons."

To demonstrate, he placed a crisp red apple on a cutting board and sliced it clean down the middle. "Here we have the fruit of the last harvest, and the seeds for the next."

"But is not yet time to plant seeds," Ogee pointed out.

"Not here in Nieuw Amsterdam. But in Israel, spring is already beginning to stir."

Earlier that day, Akiva had asked Shoshana to look

through some Jewish texts for a reading appropriate for Tu B'shvat. "Did you find something for us, Shoshana?"

"Yes, Pappa!" Shoshana ran to her room to grab the old, frayed book from her shelf. She opened the book to Psalm 96 and said, "The last few verses talk about nature." Shoshana then read aloud, first in Ladino,* then in Dutch. In turn, Ogee translated the Psalm into the Lenape language, to the best of her ability.

---

* Ladino, a combination of Hebrew and Spanish, is the language of Sephardic Jews from Portugal and Spain.

יִשְׂמְחוּ הַשָּׁמַיִם	*Let the heavens be glad,*
וְתָגֵל הָאָרֶץ	*and let the earth rejoice.*
יִרְעַם הַיָּם וּמְלֹאוֹ:	*Let the sea roar, and its fullness!*
יַעֲלֹז שָׂדַי	*Let the field and all that is in it*
וְכָל־אֲשֶׁר־בּוֹ	*exult!*
אָז יְרַנְּנוּ כָּל־עֲצֵי־יָעַר:	*Then all the trees of the woods shall*
לִפְנֵי יְדֹוָד ׀ כִּי בָא	*sing for joy before God;*
כִּי בָא	*for He comes,*
לִשְׁפֹּט הָאָרֶץ	*for He comes to judge the earth.*
יִשְׁפֹּט־תֵּבֵל	*He will judge the world with*
בְּצֶדֶק	*righteousness,*
וְעַמִּים בֶּאֱמוּנָתוֹ:	*the peoples with His truth.*

"How lovely," Sun Bird remarked.

"In our culture," So'aring Hawk added, "it is also important to honor nature, and especially the trees. Trees give so many wonderful things to our world."

"Yes, they do," Akiva chimed in. "Children, can you name some of those things?"

"Fruit!" Bina yelled.

"Nuts," the twins shouted in unison.

"Now you know why I asked you to bring fruit and nuts to our celebration," Rivka whispered to Snow Bird.

"Beauty," offered Ogee. "Some trees give us flowers in the springtime. And almost all trees help make the autumn season golden."

"What about food and shelter for birds, animals, and insects?" Shoshana suggested.

"And wood to build our homes. And fires to keep us warm and to cook our food," added Bina.

"Near our summer home, we see beavers using tree branches to build their dams," Ogee's brother pointed out.

"If we put notches in them, trees can help us find our way home. It's like having friends in the forest," said Shoshana, grinning at Ogee.

"Very good, children," Akiva said. "But we should also appreciate the hidden gifts from trees. For example, their roots help prevent soil from washing away when it rains; and after they are dead, leaves and trees decompose, which makes the forest floor fertile so more trees and other plants can grow."

"Like the wild rosebush that brought Rose and me together!" Ogee exclaimed.

The conversation turned to ways that different cultures express appreciation for trees and other types of foliage. According to Soaring Hawk, the Lenape say a prayer of thanks when they cut down a tree or burn vegetation to prepare the land for farming.

Akiva talked about Maimonides, one of the greatest Jewish thinkers who ever lived. Maimonides wrote that appreciating the natural world is the most powerful catalyst to loving God. "A catalyst," Akiva explained, "is something or someone that makes a change happen."

The two families also discovered something else in common: the moon. Each month in the Hebrew calendar begins on a full moon. When the moon is new, and completely covered by the earth's shadow, the Lenape give thanks for the gifts of creation. For instance, in May, as the sap rises in maple trees, they give thanks for maple syrup; they give thanks for strawberries in June, and for corn in August.

As everyone sat down to dinner, Shoshana began thinking about the rosebush, and how it, too, served as a catalyst—a catalyst for friendship between the Native Americans and the first Jews in North America.

Shoshana and Ogee looked at each other again and clasped hands. Without saying a word, both girls

understood that the bond they created between their families was more enduring than a living rose, sturdier than a glass rose, and more beautiful than either.

THE END

ABOUT THE AUTHOR

Robin K. Levinson has been a professional journalist since graduating from the University of New Mexico in 1981. Ms. Levinson began her career as a newspaper reporter and became a freelance writer and editor in 1993. She coauthored seven consumer-health books before shifting her concentration to Judaic topics several years ago. She is a regular contributor to *Jewish Woman Magazine* and a reviewer for *Jewish Book World*. She has won more than 30 statewide and national writing awards, including two Rockower Awards from the American Jewish Press Association. The Gali Girls series marks her debut in children's fiction. She lives in Hamilton, N.J.

ABOUT THE ILLUSTRATOR

Drusilla Kehl is a professional Illustrator working in the advertising field. She graduated with honors from Connecticut College and has traveled extensively in Africa, the Middle East and Europe. Among her many interests are history and archeology, academic art, and animal rights. She lives in New York City with her husband, a large cat, and many pet rats.